Pigwitchery

illustrated by Nathan Reed

MACMILLAN CHILDREN'S BOOKS

Pigwitch lived on a farm,
but it was no ordinary farm.

She made **marvellous** things
happen there with her magic wand.

The cow gave **chocolate milk,**

the chickens laid **rainbow-coloured eggs,**

and the cats sang in a **barbershop quartet.**

People came from miles around to see the farm.
"How wonderful!" they cried.
"How amazingly magical!"

Farmer McGee's
INCREDIBLE
Magic ☆ Farm

But then one day, Pigwitch was about to do a spell for polka-dot eggs when . . .

"Oh, no!" cried Pigwitch.
"I've lost my magic wand!"

"Maybe it's in the barn," said the cow.

"Search the pigsty," clucked the chickens.

"Have you looked in the haystack?" asked the cats.

But it wasn't in any of those places.
And without Pigwitch's magic, everything became . . .

BORING.

The cow gave plain white milk instead of chocolate.

The chickens' eggs weren't rainbow-coloured any more.

The cats miaowed instead of singing "Sweet Adeline" in perfect harmony.

"It's just an **ordinary** farm!" said the people.
"We can see one of those anywhere!"
And they all got in their cars and drove away.

Poor Farmer McGee!
No one wanted to come to his farm any more.

"We have to do something!" cried the animals.
"I'll find a new wand," decided Pigwitch.

First she tried a feather duster from the farmhouse kitchen.

ping

"Stop it!" laughed the cats.
"Oh — eek — that tickles!"

Then Pigwitch tried a twig from the rose bush.
"This would make a pretty wand," she said.

"**OUCH!**" shouted the animals.
"These flowers have all got thorns!"

whoosh

Finally Pigwitch tried an old paintbrush.
"This feels better," she said, twirling it about.

"Oh, this is hopeless!" moaned Pigwitch.
"Everything I try comes out wrong!"

"Why don't you go to the wise old pig
of the forest?" asked the cow.
"She'll know what to do!"

So Pigwitch went across the field,

down the road,

and into the **deep, dark** woods.

Beware!

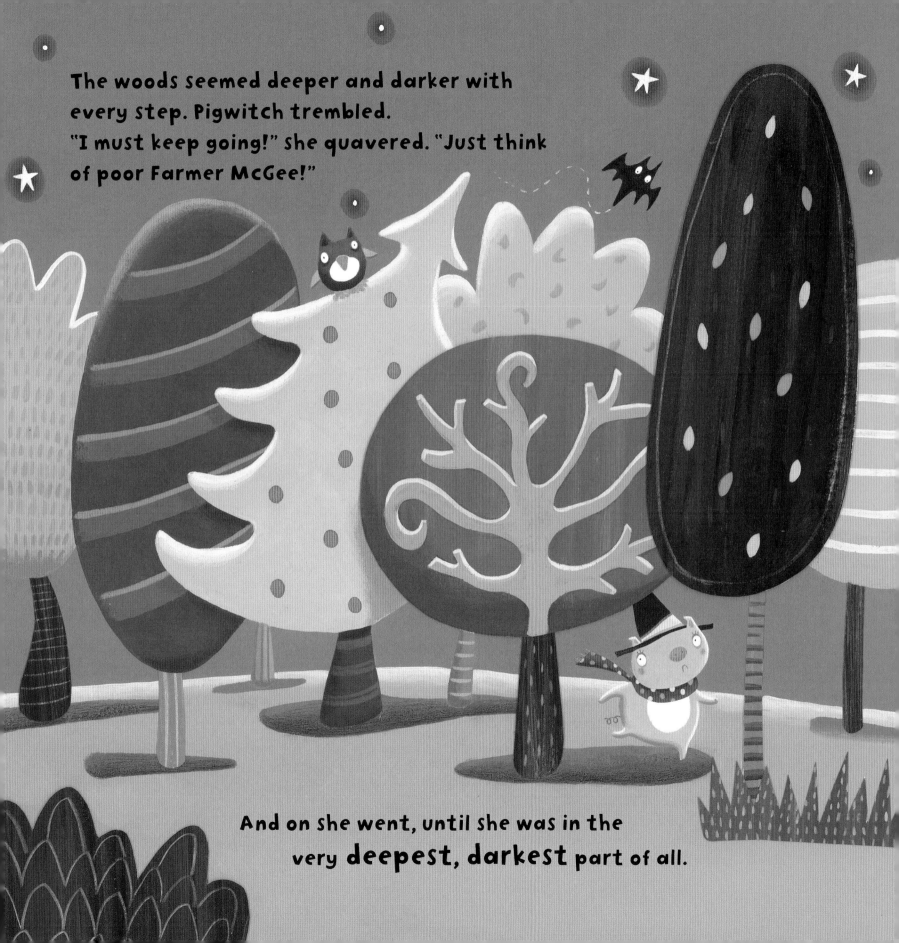

The woods seemed deeper and darker with every step. Pigwitch trembled.
"I must keep going!" she quavered. "Just think of poor Farmer McGee!"

And on she went, until she was in the very **deepest, darkest** part of all.

The wise old pig lived in a falling-down hut, and she was **very, very** old.

Pigwitch cleared her throat nervously. "Pardon me," she squeaked. "I've lost my magic wand, and I don't know what to do."

The wise old pig harrumphed. "Ridiculous!" she scoffed. "Only tiny little piglet-witches need wands! Just look behind you. All the magic you need is right there!"

Then the wise old pig went back into her hut, grumbling and mumbling to herself.

Pigwitch looked behind her.
She tried looking slowly . . .
and looking with one eye closed.

She even tried looking while she
whirled around as fast as she could,

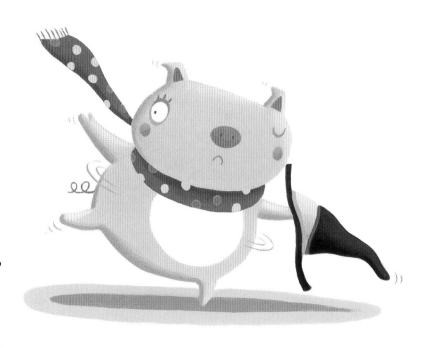

but she just got *dizzy* and fell over.

Finally Pigwitch trudged home again.

"It's no use," she said sadly. "The wise old pig said to look behind me, and I'd find all the magic I needed . . . but there's nothing there!"

"Oh dear," said the chickens.

"Hmm," said the cow, looking worried. But . . .

"Ah-ha!" shouted the cats triumphantly.

The cats strolled in a line,
waving their tails in the air.

"It's obvious!" they cried. "The wise old pig
meant that your **TAIL** is behind you! Look!"

Pigwitch peered behind her.
"But my tail's not magic!"

"**Try!**" cajoled the cats. "Everything's been so boring since you lost your wand!"

"**Try!**" begged the chickens. "We want the people to come back!"

"**Try!**" pleaded the cow. "We want Farmer McGee to be happy again!"

"Besides," they all added, **"WE MISS BEING MAGICAL!"**

So Pigwitch concentrated with all her might.

She **screwed up** her eyes,

She **hopped** on one foot,

She even **stood on her head.**

Finally, just when she had given up hope . . .

She felt a teeny, tiny spark inside her.

First it *fizzed* behind her eyes,

growing larger and **larger**.

Then it **rushed** through her tummy!

Tingled her toes!

Tickled her bottom!

And . . .

"Hurrah!" clucked the chickens.

"Oh, my goodness!" said Pigwitch.
"The wise old pig was right!
My tail does the job much better
than any wand!"

Once again, people came from miles around to see the farm.
"It's even more **wonderful** than before!" they cheered.

Farmer McGee had the
most magical
farm in the world.

And it was all because of . . .

PIGWITCHERY!

To Fiona and Julie, with love and thanks — L.W.

For Laura — N.R.

First published 2008 by Macmillan Children's Books
a division of Macmillan Publishers Limited
20 New Wharf Road, London N1 9RR
Basingstoke and Oxford
Associated companies throughout the world
www.panmacmillan.com

ISBN: 978-1-4050-9234-0 (hb)
ISBN: 978-1-4050-9318-7 (pb)

Text copyright © Lee Weatherly 2008
Illustrations copyright © Nathan Reed 2008
Moral rights asserted.

1 3 5 7 9 8 6 4 2

A CIP catalogue record for this book is available from the British Library.

Printed in Belgium by Proost